THE RIGHT ONE

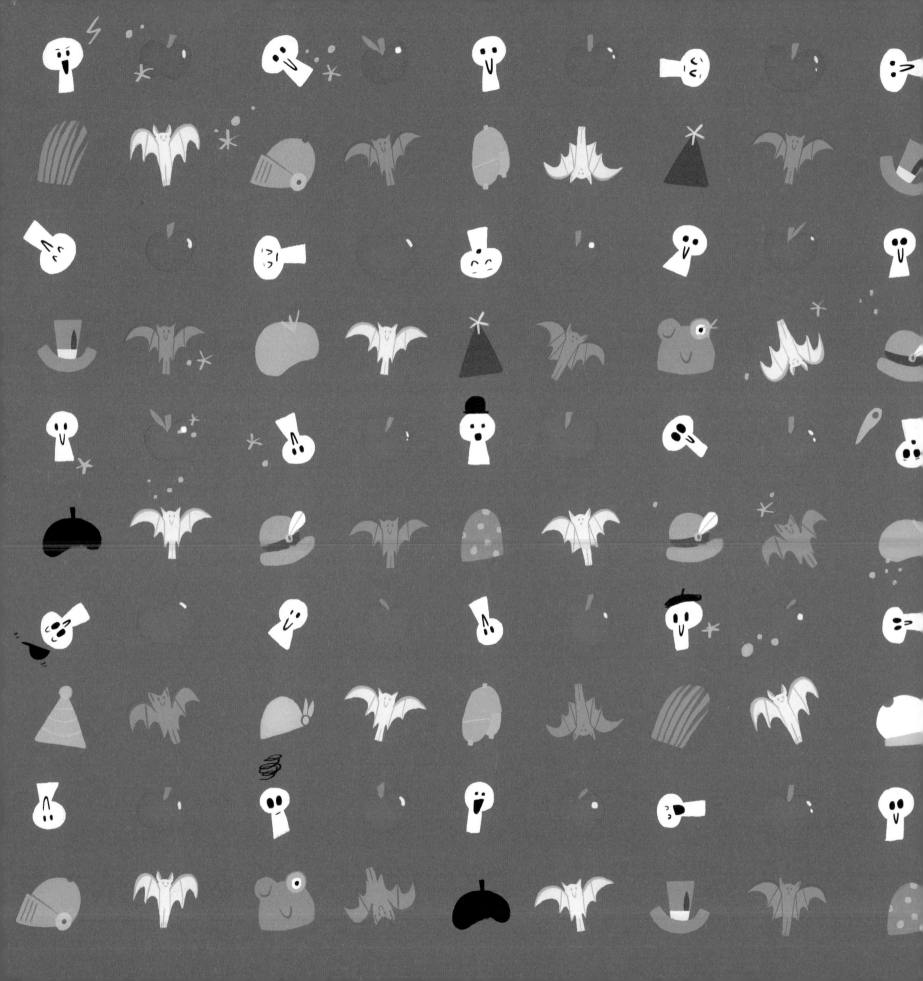

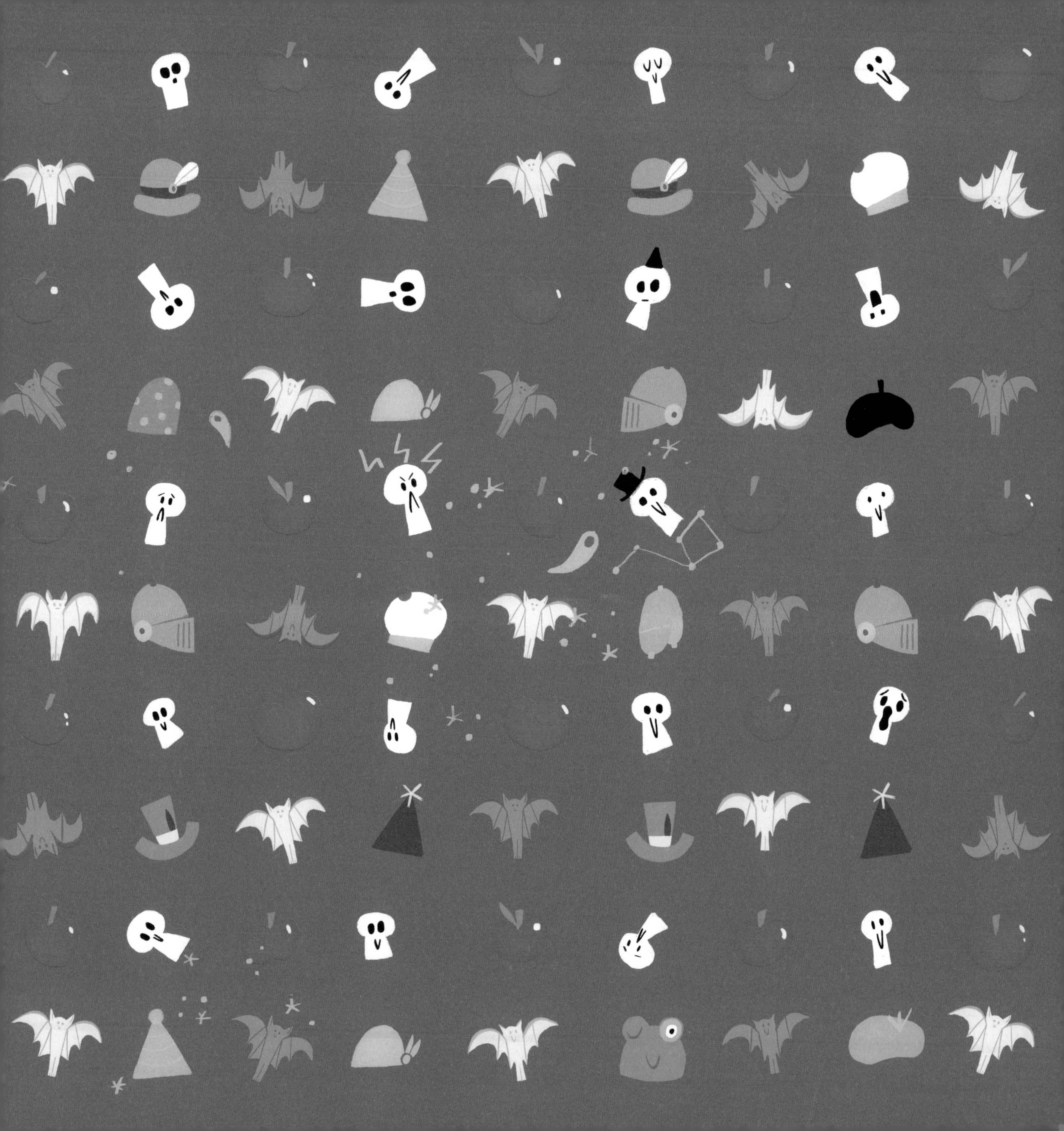

To my parents, and to Mercedes.

A TEMPLAR BOOK

First published in the UK in 2018 by Templar Publishing,
an imprint of Kings Road Publishing, part of the Bonnier Publishing Group,
The Plaza, 535 King's Road, London, SW10 0SZ
www.templarco.co.uk
www.bonnierpublishing.com

1 3 5 7 9 10 8 6 4 2

ISBN 978-1-78741-270-5

This book was typeset in Graham
The illustrations were created digitally

Edited by Katie Haworth
Designed by Olivia Cook
Publishing Director Lisa Edwards

Printed in China

THE RIGHT ONE

Violeta Noy

templar
books

Roderic was the smallest ghost
in the largest family that had ever
lived through the centuries.

You might wonder why all the ghosts in
Roderic's family look the same: it's the white sheets.
That's what ghosts **always** wear. And Roderic
wore the smallest white sheet of all.

He was also the last in a long line of Roderics . . .

which made him feel even smaller.

Most of the time, Roderic felt like his family
didn't notice he was there.

Especially when his aunts
floated right through him.

"Maybe they don't find me interesting enough,"
Roderic thought. But that could be fixed, right?

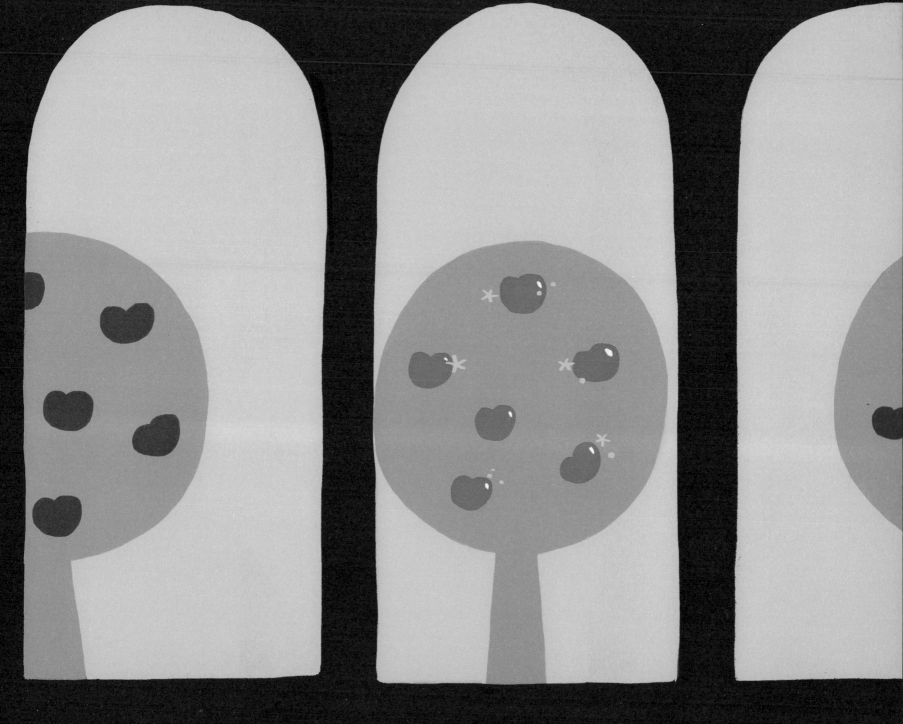

If he couldn't change his name and couldn't change his family, perhaps he could change how he looked.

He started small
and tried on a hat.

It didn't seem like much,
so he tried on another . . .

and another . . .

and another.

Roderic thought he looked fantastic, distinguished even,
but as soon as he started moving, the hats all flew away.

"Perhaps a scarf?" he thought next.
But that didn't work either.

The next morning he got bolder and put on a poncho
instead of his usual white sheet.

The colours were GREAT, but his ectoplasm
(that's what is *under* a ghost's sheet) kept showing.

So he added
some hats . . .

and a smart
bow tie.

the scarf again . . .

Finally, Roderic was ready
to show off his new look.

He was so excited!

But when he appeared at breakfast, things didn't go the way he'd planned.

His aunts didn't like his outfit . . .

and even his parents weren't convinced.

Maybe, Roderic thought,
this wasn't the place for him.

So he drifted to the city,
where he was sure everyone would
have better fashion sense.

When he got there, he waited for the
city people to notice his elegant clothes.

They didn't even see him.

Soon he felt even more
lost and invisible than
he had at home.

When his family finally found him, Roderic had
lost his beautiful outfit. They hugged and kissed him
and it felt so good to be noticed again!

When they got home, they told him they had the perfect thing for him to wear.

It was *another* white sheet.

Roderic was not happy.
The sheet still felt wrong,
so he tried on some new things.

then a handbag,
(his mum got
soooo mad)

First, he put on a rug,
(it was dusty and
made him sneeze)

then a tablecloth
(it made him smell
like mashed peas)

and even a shower curtain
(which just made him damp).

It was a
DISASTER.

A BAT

A SHEET →

GRANDMA'S FAVOURITE SKULL

Nothing felt right. It was SO FRUSTRATING!
And when ghosts get emotional,
things start to fly around.

SLIME

GRANDMA'S 2ND FAVOURITE SKULL

BOOT

BONE

It was chaos! Furniture fell over,
cupboards flew open and things that had been
lost for a very long time appeared again . . .

. . . just like the thing that landed over Roderic's head.

It smelled and swished like his old sheet.

It *was* a sheet!

But this one felt much, much better.

As soon as Roderic looked in
the mirror he knew. This was
The Right One.

He went to show his family, and this time
he had something very important to say to them:

I LIKE WEARING THIS AND I WANT TO AND I DON'T CARE IF YOU ALL WEAR WHITE SHEETS — I AM GOING TO BE DIFFERENT!!

OOOH!

And you know what?
Everybody loved it!

Because, while Roderic was
the smallest ghost in the largest family
that had ever lived through the centuries . . .

. . . that didn't mean he couldn't
teach them a thing or two.

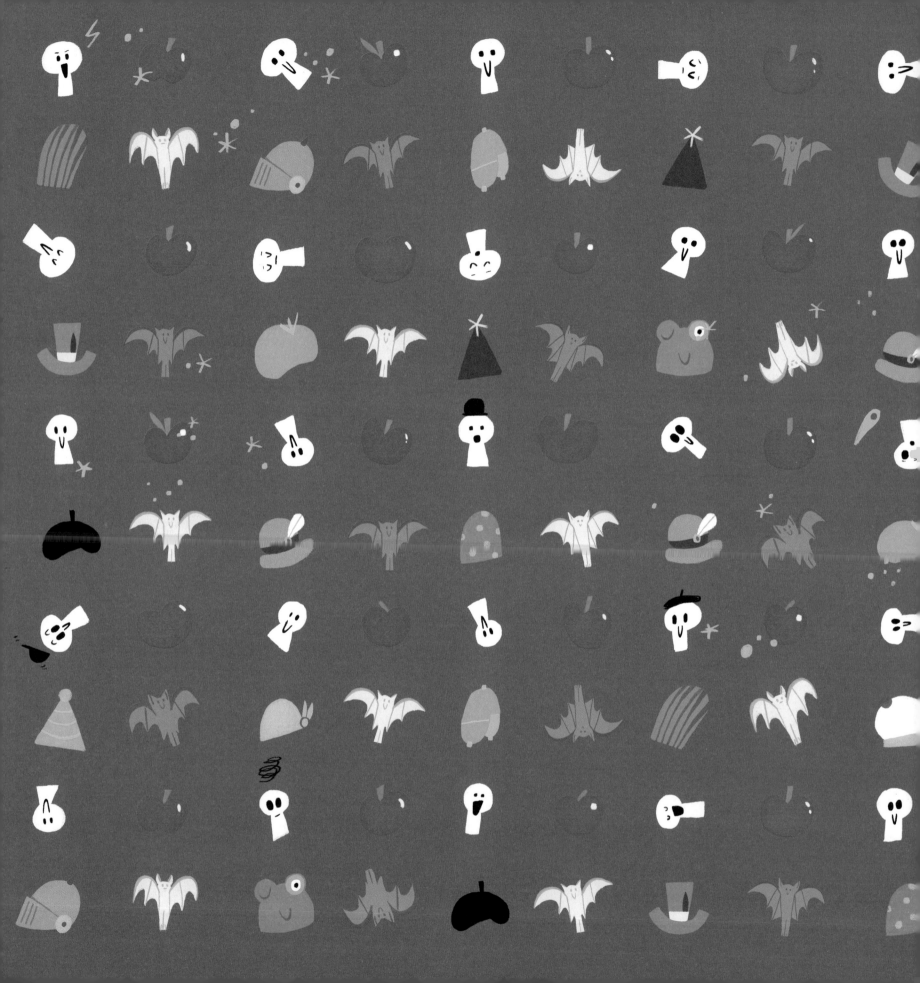

More picture books from Templar:

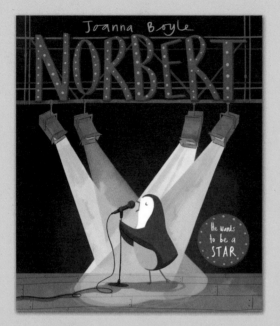

ISBN: 978-1-78741-220-0

ISBN: 978-1-78741-054-1

ISBN: 978-1-78741-234-7

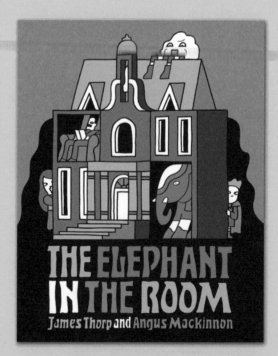

ISBN: 978-1-78370-773-7